I Want My New Shoes!

Licensed by The Illuminated Film Company
Based on the LITTLE PRINCESS animation series © The Illuminated Film Company 2007
Made under licence by Andersen Press Ltd., London
© The Illuminated Film Company/Tony Ross 2007
Design and layout © Andersen Press Ltd., 2007.
Printed and bound in China.

10   9   8   7   6   5   4

British Library Cataloguing in Publication Data available.

ISBN 978 1 84270 643 5

I Want My
New Shoes!

Tony Ross

Andersen Press · London

The Maid was
having terrible
trouble persuading
the Little Princess
to try on her new shoes.
"I don't like new shoes,"
the Little Princess shouted
crossly through the door.
"Don't be like that," soothed the Maid.
"I know you'll like them."
"No I won't!"

To the Little Princess's surprise, the
Maid popped her head through the
bedroom window and smiled.
"They're really lovely."

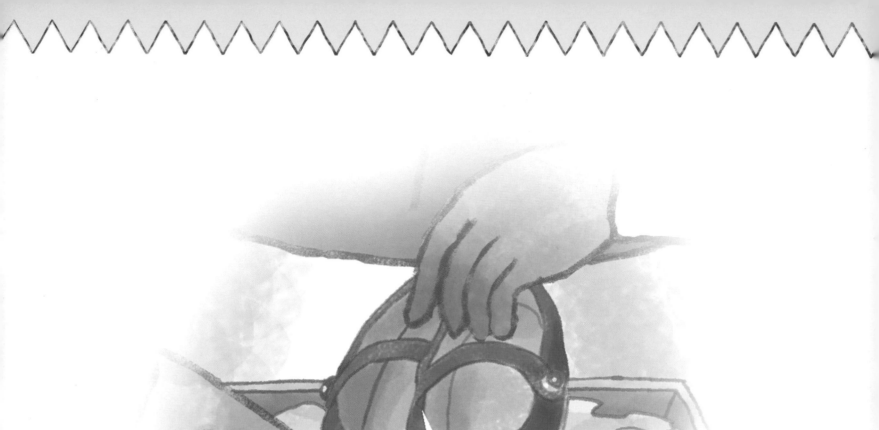

The Little Princess had to admit that the shoes did look rather lovely when the Maid lifted them out of the box.

"They won't fit," said the Little Princess half-heartedly.

The shoes were on in a jiffy.

"They fit just right," replied the Maid.

The Little Princess gasped. The shoes were perfect.

"Pretty," she whispered.

The Maid nodded. "And now they can go back in the box."

The Little Princess wasn't ready to take off her
lovely new shoes.

"But I just put them on," she argued.

"And now you can take them off again," said the Maid.

The shoes were for best only.

The Little Princess was getting crosser and crosser.

"I want to wear them!"

"But," stuttered the Maid nervously.

"NOOOOOOOoooo!"

The Little Princess screamed so loudly,
the Maid ran straight outside to find the King.

The King was in the garden playing croquet
with the General.

"She won't take them off!" panted the Maid.

The King took aim, then hit the ball with his mallet.

"As they are her shoes, I suppose she can wear them."

The ball bounced off several trees before plopping into
the Admiral's pond.

"But she'll have to look after them,"
decided the King. "She won't get
another pair if she spoils this one."

The Little Princess decided that she was never ever going to take off her new shoes. She wore them all the time, even in the bath! Dangling her foot over the side of the tub was a bit tricky, but it was worth it.

Even mealtimes were spent looking under the table at her two shiny feet. "You must see what you are eating," shouted the Chef, "it's a *tour de force!*" But the Little Princess just wasn't interested.

No one in the castle could take the Little Princess's attention away from her red shoes. Scruff and Puss had tried everything they could think of.

"Mind my shoes!" was the Little Princess's only comment, before tip-tapping upstairs.

Outside, the General called up to her window.

He was certain that he could persuade the Little Princess to come out for a gallop.

"No thank you!" answered the Little Princess. "I don't want to get my new shoes dirty."

Things were starting to go too far.
"Princess," frowned the Maid, "you
cannot wear your shoes in bed."
"They're not in bed," grinned the
Little Princess. "They are outside. See?"

The Queen stuck her crown round the door. "Sweetheart. Shoes off!"
The Little Princess climbed grumpily out of bed.
"Well I'm not leaving them on the floor!"

The new shoes were carefully placed in Puss's cat basket instead.

The next morning, the Little Princess craned out of her window to watch the others having fun in the castle grounds. She couldn't step outside, in case her new shoes got spoilt. Wearing a different pair was completely out of the question.

"I love them too much!" the Little Princess whispered. But it was very hard to stay indoors on such a nice day. A little walk outside couldn't do any harm, could it?

The Little Princess trod very carefully.

"Steady Scruff!" she shouted, when the dog bounded over to say hello.

Keeping her new shoes clean had been really quite easy so far.
Then the Prime Minister zoomed past on his tricycle.
"Hello!" he called over his shoulder, before zigzagging
all over the grass. The Little Princess laughed, then
ran after him.

The Little Princess rode her trike, played football, and went tree-climbing. Unfortunately, there were some accidents on the way.

"My washing!" cried the Maid, when the Little Princess's champion football kick swerved into the washing line. "All hands on deck!" cried the Admiral when one of the Little Princess's shoes flew into the pond. The Little Princess didn't care – she was having fun.

"Guess what?" The Maid had a surprise for the Little Princess. "You've been invited to a party."

The Little Princess hugged the invitation gleefully.

"Now you can wear your new shoes," added the Maid.

"Oh no!" gasped the Little Princess. The red shoes were covered from buckle to sole in brown, sticky mud.

The shoes were ruined. The Little Princess sat with
her head in her hands, staring sadly down at her toes.
She could never go to the party now.

The Little Princess got up and slowly walked inside.
"Bye bye shoes," she whispered. The Admiral lifted the lid
so that she could drop the dirty pair into the dustbin.

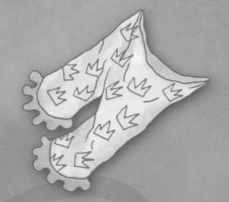

"Look at all this lot," cried the Maid, holding up the
dirty washing. "Good thing mud washes off."
The Little Princess stopped in her tracks. "Does it wash
off everything?"
The Maid nodded. "Bit of elbow grease, be good as new."
She looked down, but the Little Princess had disappeared.

"Got them!" squealed the Little Princess, when she had managed to fish the shoes out of the dustbin. She quickly found a cloth and got busy. By the time the Little Princess had finished, the shoes looked as good as new.

Now she could wear them to the party!

The Little Princess thought for a moment.

"No! Parties are too messy!"

She began to giggle. "For parties I've got…"

"... special occasion wellies!"